This book
belongs to

_____

This educational book was created in cooperation with Children's Television Workshop, producers of SESAME STREET. Children do not have to watch the television show to benefit from this book. Workshop revenues from this book will be used to help support CTW educational projects.

ON MY WAY WITH SESAME STREET

Volume 12

Just Pretend

Featuring Jim Henson's Sesame Street Muppets

Children's Television Workshop / Funk & Wagnalls

Authors

Liza Alexander
Linda Hayward
Emily Perl Kingsley
David Korr
Michaela Muntean
Pat Tornborg

Illustrators

Tom Cooke
Robert Dennis
Joe Mathieu
Kimberly A. McSparran
Maggie Swanson
Richard Walz

0-8343-0086-9

1 2 3 4 5 6 7 8 9 0

A Parents' Guide to JUST PRETEND

Children love to pretend! They think it's just fun, but children can gain a lot from imaginative play. Role-playing helps children try on other points of view. Pretending helps them explore their surroundings in their own way.

Imaginative play often starts with a few props, such as an old trunk. In "What's Up in the Attic?" Ernie and Bert turn a rainy day into a wonderful adventure through the past.

Super heroes are favorite pretend characters. "The Origins of Super-Grover" provides all the pertinent facts about Super-Grover and his powers. He's furrier than a powerful locomotive and able to leap tall sandwiches in a single bound!

"The Runaway Soup" is a silly poem about the time the neighborhood monsters got carried away.

What would Grover like to grow up to be? We find out when a magic genie in a bottle grants "Grover's Three Wishes."

Encourage your children to use their imaginations. Ask them questions such as, "What would you do if a genie gave you three wishes?" Cultivating imagination gets children on their way to enhanced creativity and a greater enjoyment of the world around them.

The Editors
SESAME STREET BOOKS

The Runaway Soup

One cold monster morning, Grover woke up and said,
"Today is a day to stay home in bed.

"But, oh, how I wish I had something hot—
A big bowl of soup would just hit the spot!"

Some hot steamy soup in a big roomy dish,
A stream of cream soup was Grover's one wish.

He knew just wishing would not do much good,
But then Grover thought of something that would.

"I will cook up some soup, I will surprise everyone,
And when they wake up, the soup will be done."

So in the biggest big pot he could find
Grover cooked up a soup that was one-of-a-kind.

"I will start with tomatoes, peppers, and peas,
Noodles and celery, peanuts and cheese...

"I will add a few pumpkins, and gooseberry jam,
Some radishes, carrots, some beans, and a yam...

"Some pancakes and pickles might taste very nice,
And what would soup be without adding some rice?"

He stirred it all up with a long wooden spoon,
Then, smiling, he said, "It should be done soon."

That soup started humming inside of the pot.
Then it started growing, and it grew a *lot*!

Over the oven and onto the floor,
That soup started heading right out the front door.

"Stop!" Grover cried. "Please do not run away!"
But that soup would not stop. That soup would not stay.

Oh, that soup-to-go was go, going, gone
On its way out the door and across the front lawn.

It bubbled along in a fat soupy stream
As each monster woke from his own monster dream.

They opened their eyes, they opened their doors,
To find runaway soup had covered their floors.

One monster hollered, and one gave a whoop,
As they all followed Grover's wild runaway soup.

It ran down Main Street and then through the back ways;
It looked like that soup could keep running for days.

But at Sesame Corner, past Alphabet Bend,
That soup missed a turn and it hit a dead end!

The monsters who followed that hot soupy path
Went slipping and sliding into a soup bath!

They had soup in their fur. They had soup-soggy clothes.
They had soup everywhere from their heads to their toes.

"Oh, no," Grover cried, "look at what I have done!"
But his friends only laughed and said, "It's been fun!

"For we've eaten soups with names that sound silly,
Like chowder, and gumbo, and pepper-pot chili,

"But we've never seen, or yet heard about,
A fast soup-to-go that could take itself out!

"So if you decide to make soup again soon,
Remind us to bring a big bowl and a spoon!"

Monster Nursery Rhymes

Old King Cookie was a merry old soul,
and a merry old soul was he.
He called for his pie, and he called for his cake,
and he called for his cookie jars three!

Oscar, Oscar, quite contrary,
how does your garden grow?
With sardine cans and old tin pans
and spider webs all in a row!

Herry had a little lamb
whose fur was monster-blue.
Wherever Herry Monster went
the monster lamb went, too.

Hey, diddle, diddle,
one cat's got a fiddle,
and a monster jumped over the moon.
A little dude laughed,
for it's so out of sight—
this party could go on till noon!

What's Up in the Attic?

It was a drizzly gray day on Sesame Street. Ernie listened to the dreary sound of the rain against the window. "There's nothing to do!" he groaned.

"Cheer up, Ern!" said Bert. "How about a game of Duckie Land? It used to be our favorite! Come on! Let's go up to the attic and find it!"

Bert gave Ernie a flashlight, and they climbed up the steep stairs to the attic door.

"Ho, hum," sighed Ernie. From the window at the top of the landing he watched the swollen rain clouds scuttle across the sky.

The windows let some light into the gloomy attic. Bert found a couple of old-fashioned lamps and turned them on.

Ernie shined his flashlight around the musty attic. "Wow!" he said, cheering up. "There's lots of great junk up here! Where's Oscar when we need him? Hee, hee!"

"Ernie," said Bert, "this is not junk. The stuff in this attic is like a scrapbook. It can tell us about our past."

Ernie knelt down beside a big old trunk. "Look at this, Bert. It's Great-Aunt Ernestine's trunk. Here's a sticker of the Eiffel Tower. That's in Paris, France."

"Wouldn't you like to travel and see the world when you grow up?" Bert asked Ernie. "*I* would."

Bert pulled a fringed jacket out of the trunk.

"This trunk is full of family things. This frontier jacket belonged to my grandfather's grandfather, old Mountain Mike. They say he once wrestled a bear to the ground with his bare hands. He had a coonskin cap, too! Let's look for it!"

"Okay, Bert," said Ernie. "A coonskin cap would be pretty neat. We could use it to play cowboy."

"And it would remind us of the old days," said Bert. "I'd look pretty sharp in a coonskin cap. Yessirree! Now, where is it?"

Ernie climbed up on a chair to poke around on top of a wardrobe. Lots of boxes were up there.

Bert dug down deeper into the trunk. "Oh, look what I found, Ernie!" cried Bert. "Uncle Bart's antique paper-clip collection!"

"Uh, what's an antique, old buddy?" asked Ernie.

"It's something very old. Some antiques are special because they're different from what we use today, and some are special because they belonged to someone important. Good old Uncle Bart! He gave me my very first paper clip," said Bert.

Ernie and Bert forgot all about looking for Duckie Land. They even forgot about the rain. But Bert did not forget about the coonskin cap. "It's got to be here somewhere!" said Bert.

Searching in a far corner, Ernie brushed aside some cobwebs and found his old tricycle. It was much too tiny for him now.

"Let's see how fast this baby can go!" He knocked past the wardrobe, and some of the hatboxes tumbled to the floor.

Then Bert discovered an old-fashioned record player called a Victrola. He put a record on it and cranked it up.

Nearby, Ernie found a fancy black jacket and a top hat, and he put them on. "May I have this dance?" he asked the dummy. They waltzed around and around to the Victrola's tinny music as Bert snapped his fingers to the beat.

"Look," said Bert. "It's Dandy the Rocking Horse. Remember what fun we had riding her when we were little?"

Bert put on Mountain Mike's jacket. He jumped into Dandy's saddle and began to sing, "Home, home on the range . . . where the deer and the antelope play . . .

"Shucks," said Bert. "I sure wish I had that coonskin cap."

Ernie slung an old brown rug over his shoulders and lumbered up behind Bert. "Grrrrrrr," he said. "I am a bear. Dare you to wrestle me to the ground like old Mountain Mike!"

"Don't be ridiculous," said Bert as he swung down off Dandy. "We've got to find that coonskin cap!"

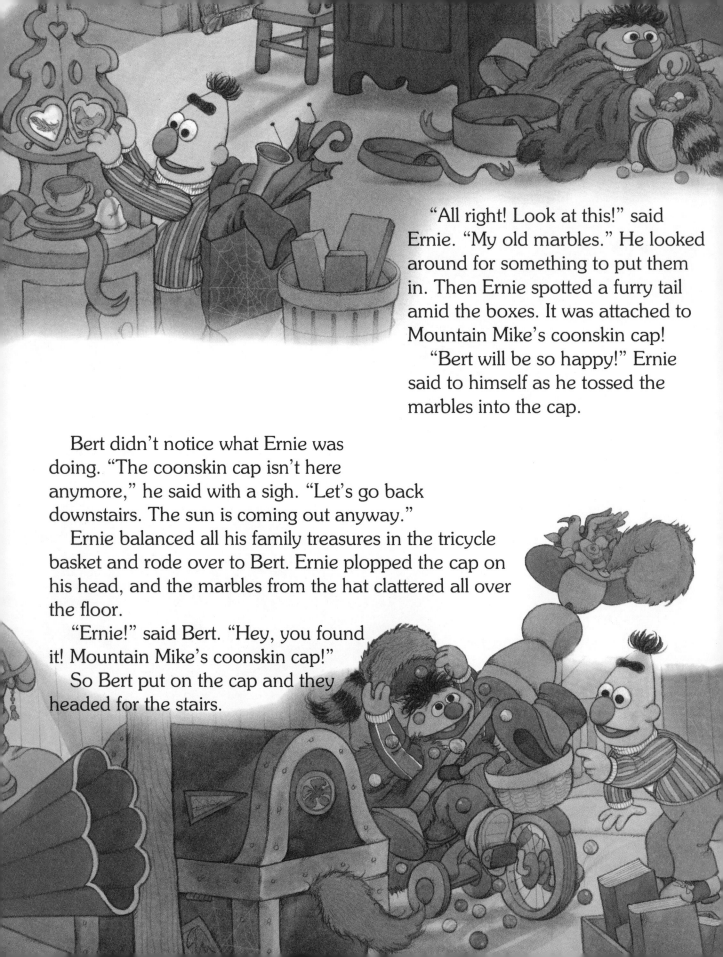

"All right! Look at this!" said Ernie. "My old marbles." He looked around for something to put them in. Then Ernie spotted a furry tail amid the boxes. It was attached to Mountain Mike's coonskin cap!

"Bert will be so happy!" Ernie said to himself as he tossed the marbles into the cap.

Bert didn't notice what Ernie was doing. "The coonskin cap isn't here anymore," he said with a sigh. "Let's go back downstairs. The sun is coming out anyway."

Ernie balanced all his family treasures in the tricycle basket and rode over to Bert. Ernie plopped the cap on his head, and the marbles from the hat clattered all over the floor.

"Ernie!" said Bert. "Hey, you found it! Mountain Mike's coonskin cap!"

So Bert put on the cap and they headed for the stairs.

"Ernie, what are you planning to do with all this junk?" asked Bert.

"This stuff is just what our place needs," said Ernie. "A dressmaker's dummy, a tiny tricycle, a top hat, and a fuzzy brown rug. Help me carry a few little things, Bert!"

So they carried all their attic discoveries down the stairs.

"This afternoon up in the attic was fun," said Ernie to Bert. "I'm glad I thought of it."

Bert just sighed.

TWIDDLE RIDDLES

Q: Where do Twiddle-bugs take the kids on Sunday afternoons?
A: To McTwiddle's for Twiddle-burgers!

Q: What do you call a Twiddle-burger that's not too small and not too big?
A: A Middle-twiddle!

Q: What does Mr. McTwiddle cook his Twiddle-burgers on?
A: A Twiddle-griddle!

Q: What do Twiddle-kiddles like best at McTwiddle's?
A: Little Twiddle-burgers with Special Twiddle Topping!

Note: Adult supervision is suggested.

Little Twiddle-burgers

To serve five—
What you need:
1 pound of ground round or chuck beef
⅓ cup of raisins
salt and pepper

What you do:
Sprinkle the raisins into the hamburger meat and twiddle the mixture with your hands until the raisins are well mixed with the meat. Make 5 flat patties, and cook them on both sides in your Twiddle-griddle, or skillet, until nice and brown. Take them out with a spatula. Put each Twiddle-burger on a sesame seed bun and spread on Special Twiddle Topping.

Special Twiddle Topping

To serve five—
What you need:
1 medium-sized zucchini squash, sliced thin
1 big golden delicious apple, quartered and sliced thin
2 tablespoons of butter or margarine
½ teaspoon of celery salt
½ teaspoon of nutmeg

What you do:
Melt the butter or margarine in a skillet, and put in the squash and apple slices. Cover the skillet. Cook the squash and apples for about 7 minutes, or until they're soft, stirring them once in a while. Stir in the seasonings. Now the Special Twiddle Topping is ready to be spread on your Twiddle-burgers.

Q: What do you call boys and girls who love Twiddle-burgers?
A: Twiddle-kiddles!

The Disappearing Act

What's missing?

What's missing now?

What's missing this time?

Grover's Three Wishes

Because you let me out of this bottle...

...I grant you three wishes.

Gee, let me see. What would Grover like to be?

Point to Grover,
the sea captain.

I wish I were a brave sea captain.

Point to Grover,
the baseball star.

GO GROVER

I wish I were a baseball star.

Point to Grover, the rodeo rider.

I wish I could ride in a rodeo.

3

"Wishing is so much fun, but I am glad to be just lovable furry old Grover!"

The Origins of Super-Grover

Where did Super-Grover come from? How did he get his super-powers? To answer these questions, we must go back in history . . . back to the time when Grover was a very little monster.

One day Grover's mommy said to him, "Well, Grover, it is almost Halloween. I had better start making your costume. Now, let me see what I have. . . ." She found an old towel, a funny old helmet that Grover's daddy had once brought home, and a few other odds and ends.

She worked and worked, and finally she announced, "Well, I have finished your costume, Grover. Just in time for Halloween. I hope you like it!"

"Why, Mommy!" cried Grover with delight. "It is a super-hero costume! Just what I wanted."

Then Grover thought of something. "Oh, dear," he said. "I must find a telephone booth so that I can put on my costume. Super-heroes always change into their costumes in telephone booths. I'll run down to the one on the corner."

From that time on, Grover found that whenever he put on his super-hero Halloween costume, he changed from mild-mannered plain little Grover Monster into brave and fearless . . . SUPER-GROVER . . .

... SMARTER THAN A SPEEDING BULLET...

... FURRIER THAN A POWERFUL LOCOMOTIVE...

... ABLE TO LEAP TALL SANDWICHES IN A SINGLE BOUND !!!

✳ SUPER-GROVER'S SUPER-POWERS ✳

IMPORTANT: EVEN IF YOUR MOMMY MAKES YOU A SUPER-HERO COSTUME, **DO NOT** TRY TO DO THESE THINGS. YOU CANNOT HAVE SUPER-POWERS. THERE IS ONLY ONE SUPER-GROVER.

PRAIRIE DAWN'S UPSIDE-DOWN POEM

UP is where we have to go
To go away from DOWN.
But what if everything were turned
The other way around?

Floors would then our ceilings be,
And ceilings be our floors.
But would we then go DOWN the stairs,
To go through attic doors?

Sitting DOWN would seem quite strange,
And standing UP would, too.
And would the birds go underground
If UP is where they flew?

What would saying "bottom" mean?
Would mountains still have tops?
Would rabbits, frogs and kangaroos
Have trouble with their hops?

Falling DOWN I do a lot.
Would falling UP hurt less?
If UP were DOWN would spilling milk
Produce a smaller mess?

All these things I'm wondering
Are silly, without doubt.
But how do you suppose we'd feel,
With things turned...inside out?